The Very Noisy Night

Diana Hendry   Jane Chapman

LITTLE TIGER PRESS

It was the middle of the night, and Big Mouse was fast asleep in his big bed. Little Mouse was wide awake in his little bed.

"Big Mouse! Big Mouse!" called Little Mouse. "I can hear something rushing around the house, huffing and puffing."

Big Mouse opened one eye and lifted
one ear. "It's only the wind," he said.

"Can I come into your bed?"
asked Little Mouse.
     "No," said Big Mouse. "There isn't room."
And he turned over and went back to sleep.

Little Mouse lay listening
to the wind. Then, suddenly,
between a huff and a puff,
came a . . .

TAP   TAP   TAP
TAP

Little Mouse climbed out of bed, opened
the front door—just a crack—and peeped out.

WHOOOSH!

went the wind, but there was no one outside. "Big Mouse! Big Mouse!" called Little Mouse. "I can hear someone tapping. I think there's a burglar on the roof."

Big Mouse got out of
bed and opened the bedroom
curtains. "Look," he said, "it's
only a branch tapping on the
window. Go back to sleep."

"Can I come into your bed?"
asked Little Mouse.

"No," said Big Mouse. "You
wriggle."

Little Mouse lay in
his own bed and listened
to the wind huffing and
puffing and the branch
tap-tapping—and someone
calling,

"HOO-HOO!
HOO-HOO!"

Little Mouse climbed out of bed again. This time he looked under it. Then he looked in the wardrobe, and feeling very frightened, he yelled, "Big Mouse! Big Mouse! I think there's a ghost in the room, and it's looking for someone. It keeps calling, 'Who-who, who-who!' "

Big Mouse sighed, sat up, and listened. "It's only an owl," he said. "It stays up all night, like you."

"Can I come into your bed?" asked Little Mouse.

"No," said Big Mouse. "Your paws are always cold." Big Mouse pulled the blanket over his head and went back to sleep, and Little Mouse got back into his own bed.

Little Mouse sat up
and listened to the wind
huffing and puffing, and
the branch tap-tapping,
and the owl hooting.
But shhh!
What was that?

DRIP DRIP DRIP DRIP

"Big Mouse! Big Mouse!" he
called. "I think it's raining inside."
And Little Mouse jumped out of bed
and fetched his red umbrella.

Big Mouse got out of bed, too. He opened the front
door to see if it was raining at all. Then Big Mouse went
into the kitchen and turned off the dripping faucet. He
gently pried the umbrella out of Little Mouse's paws and
put it away.

"Can I come into your bed?"
asked Little Mouse.

"No, you're nice and snug in your own
bed," said Big Mouse, taking him back to the bedroom.

Little Mouse lay and
listened to the wind huffing
and puffing, the branch
tap-tapping, and the owl
hooting. And just as he was
beginning to feel very sleepy
indeed, he heard . . .

"WHEEE, WHEEE, WHEEEEE!"

"Big Mouse! Big Mouse!" he called. "You're snoring."

Wearily, Big Mouse got up. He put his earmuffs on Little Mouse's ears. He put a paper clip on his own nose, and he went back to bed.

Little Mouse lay and listened to—n o t h i n g!
It was very, very, very quiet. He couldn't hear
the wind huffing or the branch tapping or the owl
hooting or Big Mouse snoring. It was so quiet that
Little Mouse felt he was all alone in the world.

He took off the earmuffs. He got out of bed
and pulled the paper clip off Big Mouse's nose.
"Big Mouse! Big Mouse!" he cried. "I'm lonely!"

Big Mouse flung back his
blanket. "Better come into
my bed," he said. So Little
Mouse hopped in, and his
paws were cold . . .

and he needed just
a little wriggle before
he fell fast asleep.

Big Mouse lay and listened to the wind huffing and puffing and the branch tap-tapping and the owl hooting and Little Mouse snuffling, and very soon he heard the birds waking up. But neither of them heard the alarm clock . . .

BECAUSE THEY WERE
BOTH FAST ASLEEP!

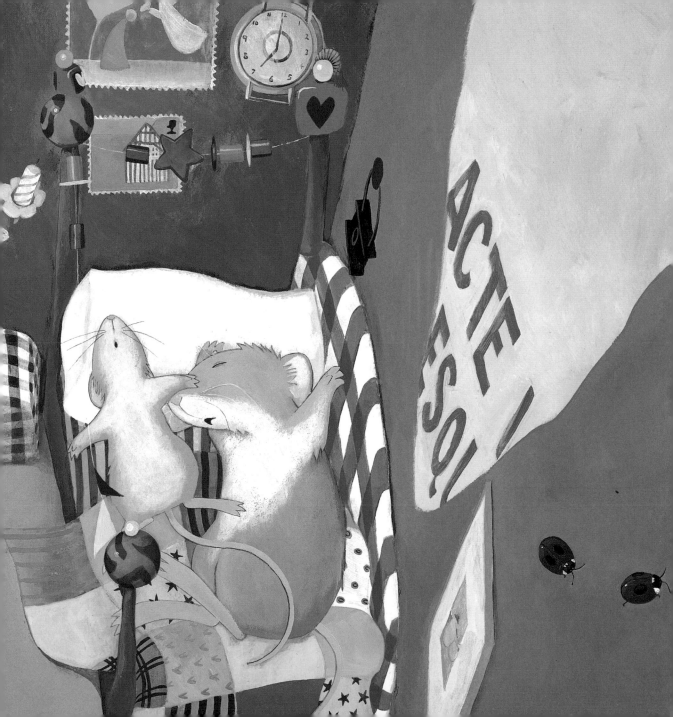

For Emelia, with love
— D.H.

For Anthony, Jane, Mark,
Katy and Alice, with love
— J.C.

This edition produced 2004 for Scholastic Inc.
557 Broadway, New York, NY 10012 by
Little Tiger Press, an imprint of Magi Publications
1 The Coda Centre, 189 Munster Road, London SW6 6AW, UK
www.littletigerpress.com
First published in Great Britain 1999 by Little Tiger Press
Text © Diana Hendry, 1999 · Illustrations © Jane Chapman, 1999
· Printed in China · ISBN 1 84506 146 2
1 3 5 7 9 10 8 6 4 2